THE CHILDREN SPEAK

THE AGE THAT I AM

Andrew Marshall Jr.

Author's Tranquility Press
ATLANTA, GEORGIA

Copyright © 2024 by Andrew Marshall Jr.

All rights reserved. No part of this publication may be reproduced, distributed or transmitted in any form or by any means, including photocopying, recording, or other electronic or mechanical methods, without the prior written permission of the publisher, except in the case of brief quotations embodied in critical reviews and certain other noncommercial uses permitted by copyright law. For permission requests, write to the publisher, addressed "Attention: Permissions Coordinator," at the address below.

Andrew Marshall Jr./Author's Tranquility Press
3900 N Commerce Dr. Suite 300 #1255
Atlanta, GA 30344, USA
www.authorstranquilitypress.com

Ordering Information:
Quantity sales. Special discounts are available on quantity purchases by corporations, associations, and others. For details, contact the "Special Sales Department" at the address above.

The Children Speak: The Age That I Am /Andrew Marshall Jr.
Paperback: 978-1-964810-60-7
eBook: 978-1-964810-40-9

About The Author

Andrew Marshall, Jr. was born and raised in Columbus, Georgia, and also attended Claflin Elementary School, a formerly segregated public school that is approximately 145 years old. Claflin Elementary School consisted of grades kindergarten through sixth. Coincidentally, the Author's father, Andrew Marshall, Sr., also attended Claflin as a child growing up in Columbus. Andrew Marshall, Jr., was a student in the last sixth grade class at Claflin, immediately prior to Columbus, Georgia experiencing mandated integration of this Nation's public-school systems.

In June 1976, after completing his junior year, the Author graduated from high school. In December of the same year, when he was still 17 years old, Andrew enlisted in the United States Marine Corps (USMC). Prior to leaving for Boot Camp, he made an attempt to count every house and/or lots (where a home had once stood) that he could remember having lived during his upbringing. Subsequently, he counted 13 different home locations. After conferring with an older sister on this number, that sister told him that he had missed two other houses. The Author is capable of recalling practically every day of his life.

Andrew Marshall, Jr. had a once in a lifetime experience when he met and conversed with one of history's greatest literary giants of poetry, Miss Gwendolyn Brooks, who was the first African American to win the Pulitzer Prize for her book Annie Allen (poetry). Reverently, this chance meeting and brief discussions with Miss Gwendolyn Brooks have been the motivation for some of Andrew Marshall, Jr., more poignant allegorical and metaphorical writings (satirical as well). Additionally, this Author has historically embraced the writings of Langston Hughes, Paul Lawrence Dunbar, along with many of the other notable Harlem Renaissance Writers. With respect to this literary field of endeavors, Andrew Marshall, Jr. has read and/or attempted to analyze the works of many other authors, whether contemporary or historical.

Andrew Marshall, Jr., graduated in 1983 with honors from Bethune-Cookman University (formerly, "Bethune-Cookman College"), an *HBCU* or Historically Black College or University. After graduating from Bethune-Cookman, Andrew Marshall, Jr. completed a Master of Science degree in Human Resources Management and Development at National Louis University. He retired from the United States Federal Government. He is a member of Kappa Alpha Psi Fraternity, Incorporated.

Dedication

This book is being dedicated to All of the Children, Everywhere.

The Age That I AM

The Age That I AM Is *The Age That I AM.*

Children mustn't ever have to always cram.

Let them know that Your love's forever free,

And give them Your Time most consistently.

Give them ample space to Shine and strive,

Some late bloomers will take a longer while.

Never put their dreams up for Life's remand,

Teach with Patience They might Understand.

The children aren't Pawns that you Sacrifice.

We must adhere to Love's most godly advice:

Patience, Time and Love are Lifelong Virtues,

Because Life comes with its own set Curfews.

CAN'T!

Can't never can and never Could!

Can't be forever up to No GOOD!

Can't cannot be a friend of TIME!

Can't lag and stay too far behind!

Can't act like Can't's good friend!

Can't sink all in the deepest end!

Can't Can't and neither can You!

Can't won't tell what one can do!

Open The Door!

What time does Heaven open its *Door?*

Who's invited to come back in for more?

Does Heaven forgive the Life of Sinner?

Or must one hold the ticket of a winner?

What time does Heaven open the Door?

Eye of the needle widened for the poor?

What time does Heaven open the Door?

Once beautiful *Life* is now just eye sore?

What if Tomorrow Never Comes?

What if Tomorrow Never Comes?

To continue the wait makes me dumb?

What if Tomorrow Never Comes?

Do My hopeful feelings become numb?

What if Tomorrow Never Comes?

Does adding and subtracting net none?

What if Tomorrow Never Comes?

Will Dream Home remain in The Slum?

We Who Own The Night

We Who Own The Night
Must Barter With Each Passing Day,
Then Continually Subtract Our Time,
From The Barterer's Delinquent Pay.

We Who Own The Night
Know That Time Can Be Taken Away,
Traveling Along Life's Foggy Distance,
The *Toll* Charges For Premature Gray.

Time Out For Talking

You get a Lifetime out for talking.

Talking is a way of word stalking.

Talking makes Life appear *Sane.*

Talking makes a deficit your gain.

Talking is *Loquacious* way to flee.

Talking is what Blind People See.

Talking lets the *Echoes* talk back.

Talking is being in Red, not Black.

Teaching And Learning

Teaching And Learning are one conjoined twin,

Both connected to the same Purpose And End.

Teach the children what the need to truly Know,

Children will learn to live, whether Fast or Slow.

Mysterious Ways

Rain floods a watered soul in their tracks.

There is shelter after dark skies collapse.

Hope is to find the straight road for home,

Life must not drown with swimmer's roam.

Clouds do drench after alarming their sky,

Changes in an instance, living knows why.

Then Light the world with Hellish matches,

The Rainbow comes then Heaven relaxes.

Naught For All

Naught Means Nothing,

And gives nothing to All.

Naught is forever *Short,*

Wanting to stand up tall.

Naught is always giving,

Then Naught is only left.

Naught is having *naught,*

All given to *Naughty Self.*

Naught is empty pockets,

Deep, dusty, oh so mean!

Naught is the eye sockets,

Seeing *Naught* in a dream.

Storm Twister

Help Me Help You Help Yourself
You can't walk through life with a bent knee.
You must strive for everybody to live *as free*.
Plant your seed and let love's success grow.
Your timbered Tree will swing back and forth.

Help Me Help You Help Yourself
Life will flourish with a true and focused heart.
Just give your best while taking your *Fair part.*
Fear not for the wind shall discriminately blow,
Find the gold stashed away for y*our Rainbow.*

The Marathon Runner

Life runs the race, pitting straight ahead,

Like time is competing with its Marathon,

At times moving with The Speed of Dred,

Sometimes snailing with fractured Inches.

The Marathon Runner will move the pace,

According to runner Gambit and Trenches.

Black Cat Jazz

I want one full life for each of *My Lives!*
The Black Cat doesn't talk Jazzy Jives!

Day Breaks for Night

While The Moon circles the earth,

Day and Night will both give birth.

The Night shadow's seen by Day,

The Day then Stalks Nightly Prey.

Selfish of Love

Love doesn't love anyone,

When love is being its unlovable self.

While love has no overflow,

Time keeps the memories that love left.

When Will The Rain Stop?

When will the rain stop?

Rain is hunger and the child counts each drop.

When will the rain stop?

Rain is a dirt floor that a child cannot ever mop.

When will the rain stop?

Rain floods a child like a barren, seedless crop.

When will the rain stop?

Rain is a biscuit and gravy that empty plate sop.

Bubble

Love can make you do some things

You might've pledged to once again,

Never Do.

Like attempting to walk through LIFE,

Talking with swollen gum then MUST-

Now chew.

Walk Proud

Walk Proud

When the road is long and narrow.

Walk Proud

When looking at the loaded barrel.

Walk Proud

When a dream is farther than near.

Walk Proud

When an echo's the voice you hear.

Walk Proud

When rain floods the little bare feet.

Walk Proud

When the mirror loves you will greet.

The Bell

The Bell rings to end your deepest sleep.

Dreams are awakened for Souls to keep.

Nothing worthy is ever given freely away.

For all Life desires there is a price to pay.

Start the day befriending the likes of you,

And keep this friend close all life through.

Nothing worthy is ever given freely away.

Make your own Life do the good you say.

The Children Speak

1. The Children Speak of lost Love that might never be found loving again.
2. The Children Speak of being blamed for worldly sin.
3. The Children Speak in a language frozen to some tongues.
4. The Children Speak of their own Kingdom they must make come.
5. The Children Speak of Liberation that's free from Life's chains.
6. The Children Speak of a Freedom only they can attain.
7. The Children Speak of revenge and avenging their own.
8. The Children Speak of lost time that is now forever gone.
9. The Children Speak of Traveling the paved Road to Death.
10. The Children Speak of riches but receive the pyrite glittering wealth.
11. The Children Speak from the memory that remembrance forgot.
12. The Children Speak of having nothing and being labeled the have nots.
13. The Children Speak of being muted and using braille to see.
14. The Children Speak of the systemic plot perpetrated against thee.
15. The Children Speak of envy that jealousy has perfected.

16. The Children Speak of seeking opportunities only to be rejected.
17. The Children Speak of education and promoting their self-worth.
18. The Children Speak of living in harmony on The Indigenous earth.
19. The Children Speak of respect for their individual talents.
20. The Children Speak of the pressures to always remain strong and valiant.
21. The Children Speak of misguided teachings with words that do not always translate.
22. The Children Speak of arriving early but being counted late.
23. The Children Speak of dreams that most won't understand.
24. The Children Speak of their dreams dying from constant remand.
25. The Children Speak of Love that does not sway.
26. The Children Speak of a bright future after living yesterday.
27. The Children Speak of the dark days that come out at night.
28. The Children Speak of dining with dead presidents to satisfy an insatiable appetite.

Where?

Where must we go away from Here?

Where can people dance and cheer?

Where do Dark Days look for Sunny?

Where's the table serving US Funny?

Where is Heaven for love never free?

Where's the Chariot, late bus for Me?

America, To Me (The Dissertation)

America means the world to me. America shines from sea to sea. Dreams that reach the sky so high, America conquers the heavenly sky. America contains All yearning dreams, America watches as Twilight Gleams. WE The People under One Nation, The Gavel must be fair without hesitation. The selected home where Freedom lives, And every diner gets to deal. A love for Justice that is True, Where Equality is spread evenly, not on just a select few. When America's Trumpet sounds its alarm, All Citizens are protected from harm. A Peaceful Home of The Brave and Land of the free. This is what America must also mean for Me.

The Whistle Blows....

The whistle blows....

It is now time to get all the way up.

Too much sleep gives Life hiccups.

Sleep will only comfort itself in bed.

Sleep's what awakens *Must Dread.*

The Melanted Seeds

Time has melanted life's Rainbow with darkest Clouds,

That can always perdict a pouring rain storm and snow.

Like the coming floods that drown flowers in the bosom -

BELOW!

Melanted Seeds are fertilized ovaries that may never get

To Grow.

Their Turn

Freedom Says,

You must not water down the Children,

So, give a life warning to them straight:

Their turn in life's detoured and bended,

Now, they will have to take it or just wait.

My Time to Shine

My time to shine is

Before the dawn of each day.

My time to shine is

The light that shows My way.

My time to shine is

Knowing that I'm envy's wish.

My time to shine is

Freedom not undistinguished.

Hole

Can't fall into another hole

That You cannot crawl out.

The hole can encircle a life,

The Hole is a taker of Clout.

Trust (a poem for Trey Trey)

Withstand the Sun's different shines!

And, Then:

Do cherish the rising of the lovely sun,

While I look for shade before its setting.

The pure heart of the child shall mellow,

On this understanding I am now betting.

The sun goes down and darkness rules.

Losses and wins are chances you take.

Birth and death should be one friend.

The greatness of man is not a mistake.

The darkest hours of your life journey,

A crescent moon provides ample light.

Great timber knows the hope of a tree,

Rejoice in the will to embrace a Night.

What would this world forever grieve,

Without the life commissioned for us?

While learning can be a painful plight,

Growing is more agony when you rush.

Fill your heart with true destinations,
Over horizons only death must entrust.
This world could have never become,
Except for the time God gives in *Trust.*

Love Child

Love to a child is like candy to a baby,

A Mother's milk that is lovingly poured.

And Love without nurturing is *today be,*

The bitterness that shall not be adored.

The People Arrival

No person has truly arrived

Until their People get there.

When The People all arrive,

Love will have paid the fare.

Stalking

Stalk the good life and true love for each other.

Stalk for the Children, Their Father and Mother.

This way of stalking is never charged for Crime.

Stalk like a repossessor coming to *Get All Mine.*

Love And Life

Believe in a Love as great as Yourself.

Believe that Love has one Last Breath.

Believe in a Love that can live Forever.

Believe that Love and Life *Both Clever.*

Take Me Under Your Wings

Take Me Under Your Wings,
And guide me towards the sky,
I am Love's youngest dove,
Now My wish is to fly.

Take Me Under Your Wings,
Gently push me from your nest,
With the strongest wind of desire,
I shall always do my truly best.

Take Me Under Your Wings,
Never ever being blinded by the sun,
I will honor your prevalent prayers,
My gifted wings are flighty and done.

Take Me Under Your Wings,
The moon and stars I will footstool.
As Life takes the first virgin flight,
Pray that my air time isn't cruel.

The Dream I Have

The Dream I Have

Makes Freedom Free.

The Dream I Have

Dreams of freeing ME.

Crawl Stroke

Life sometimes rumble like a river and roar isn't heard,

Yet makes all repeat their own adjective-laden adverbs.

The river consummates living with hot waters and leaks,

Rainbow comes after flooding reaches its highest peak.

Sometimes everyone must learn to do their crawl stroke,

Hands back and forth, praying cold waters will not choke.

Life is not unlike the polluted that buries the good soil too,

Life itself shows no respect for a person, nor what you do.

Once heavenly clean waters now flow into a Sinking Life,

And Life can be like the river, drowning for one salty slice,

A tiring cruelty that lets fear and hope charge a Hefty Fee,

To crawl, stroke to wherever living is calm and Flood Free.

Piece of Sleep

I want to wake on up,

Then get paid.

I want peace in sleep,

Before I'm laid.

Sun Rising

The sun sits at noon,

Then sets off on an evening burn.

Rises again in morn',

Before taking another *Hotter Turn.*

Collaborators

The red bird and blue bird joined forces

To dig up deliciously tasting earthworms,

But met with watchful eyed bumble bees

Who attack invaders in *Stinging Swarms.*

THE FREEDOM SPEAKER

I WANT ALL THAT WAS MINE,
AND I WILL TAKE MINE NOW!
(THE FREEDOM SPEAKER IS
GLUTTON FOR JUSTICE AND
EYES ARE ABOVE THE BROW)

From The Top of The Mountain

From the Top of The Mountain,

I can observe the world's endless terrain.

From the Top of The Mountain,

I can hitch a ride on a grounded Airplane.

Lone Traveling With One Befriended

I take the Road that leads to You.

However narrow, the Way is True.

The Road may wind and do bend,

Never traveling alone with friends.

Grace

If I could move a great mountain,

By raising just One of My Hands,

This deserted world never perish

In the sinking grips of Quicksand.

The ocean would drown in waves,

Swimmer is Pardoned and Saved.

All I Want (The Hands of Time)

All I want is a little piece of *My* mind.

All I want is hands that tell *Real* time.

Time

Where Do All of Life's Good Times Go?

Time moves a dream from bad to slow?

If Time could talk, What does Time say?

Will Time Tell US the Right Time of day?

Or spent Time on the road to be paved?

Any Time wasted cannot ever be saved!

Bitter Cakes

The children do not have bread to eat,

And Life has baked them Bitter Cakes.

God did not make such a bad Mistake.

Lest We forget the Prayers that repeat.

In Abundance

In Abundance

Life gives and also takes.

In Abundance

We sleep 'til hourly wakes.

In Abundance Dream of freedom's home.

In Abundance

Never will be left all along.

In Abundance

We die before time awake.

In Abundance

Life is grounded in forsake.

Something For Everybody To See

I am my gift to show the whole wide world,
I am something for love to keep and adore.
My gift is beautifully wrapped for All to see,
The shining light that does not dim on thee.

A picture of my uniqueness you see on film.
My story's beholden to any critics or friends.
I am the first of the last who's yet to be seen.
I am the hope and the prophecy of A Dream.

Paint Me The Color of Love

Paint Me The Color of Love,

For I Am The Masterpiece that Life cannot ever ignore.

Brush up my imperfections with all the Scrubber might.

Make my frame molded perfectly for the world's delight.

Make my eyes beam with the light of the sparkling stars,

Give the vision to see my destination from a distant afar.

Braid my hair in heaven's loveliest and twisted cornrows,

Like the wind that moves with time, watch the love flows.

Now picture The Creator unmistakable and Loving finest,

Made by the hands of the eternal and forever the divinest.

Paint Me The Color of Love and let My paint dip into core,

I am The Masterpiece life cannot accept but forever adore.

Light Up The World

Light Up The World
With a lovely smile to greet New Life each day.
Let your light shine to show you the Right Way.
Smile with confidence that'll make a Day beam.
Let your smile foretell of the dreams you dream.
Sometimes your smile must disguise Life's hurt.
Still, make your smile put any doubt on the alert.

The Motherless Children

Why must life consummate the motherless Love child?

Is it to just let them run and chase their other twin wild?

The motherless children are inseparable living together.

They bond like the poorly knitted and worn out sweater.

The motherless children find comfort in dying with them.

The motherless children swallow their cold-weather film.

The Fatherless Child

The fatherless child will blame the mother

Who must raise both sisters and brothers.

The fatherless child learns what they keep.

The fatherless child fears while they weep.

The fatherless child blames the cruel world.

The fatherless child spins and lets life twirls.

The fatherless child makes up own life laws.

The fatherless child gets caught in the jaws.

The fatherless child has a blank, dark stare.

The fatherless child fights and doesn't care,

The fatherless child believes all hates them.

The fatherless child becomes life's synonym.

One Minute

Going another minute is not out of the way.

One minute of your time is never a full *Day*.

One minute can begin the start of a lifetime.

One minute can also be love and life divine.

Rain

Even if the rain would please and just go away,

Rain has a place where it always seems to stay.

Rain knows the quickest route back to its home.

Rain and roads have been paved to flood alone.

Freedom's Call

Give Me My Freedom,

Before taking My everlasting, last breath.

I must know that I have no more time left.

Give Me My Freedom,

And give *this* Freedom to *The People All.*

Let Freedom answer when Freedom Call.

Camouflage

Life is not easy when wearing the defiant camouflage, Whose colors must constantly change from bright pastel to defiant dark. Life can reduce living to becoming like a chameleon whose telescopic eyes swell, while repetition masks its submissive grin. Only the chameleon knows if changing colors is real or just pretending.

Cane Sugar And Raw Salt

Sugar and Salt appear non discerningly alike.

When seen with measuring eyes, both *Bright.*

Both boil after becoming simmered or heated.

Both are the systems of life's deadly diabetes.

Both often look identical, mirroring each other.

They are likened to kin, but love being *Nother.*

Dark Days

You swear that rain loves me,

And this might be true.

But my sun loves you,

And will make dark days blue.

Comin' To get You

Caller Sayin'
Little children are outside playin'
Early night is now dayin'

Caller Sayin'
All on their knees
They now must be prayin'

Caller Sayin',
On parents owed debt,
Children are payin'.

Caller Sayin'
Darlings precious lives
Will never be grayin'

Caller Sayin'
Releasing balloons
Misgambled the parlayin'

No Beef With Nobody

Jail's an injustice: *Barrel of Pork!*

Sing Sing still Sings in New York.

Snatch and Grab for Daily Bread,

Freezing until Your ribs are Dead.

Prison slabs are served iced cold,

Forgotten life of Rebellious Souls.

M-E Too Movement

I got mine,

Now you get your.

I slept in my own bed,

Without bed sores.

You got mine,

And was spoon fed,

Life can be very scary,

But don't be afraid.

Knowing

Don't believe in believing,

Because believing is blindly growing.

Don't believe in believing,

Because believing is never knowing.

A Change of Scenery

When you need a Change of Scenery,

Visit the one place where you find You.

A place that is always near yet very far,

Then, You will know just where You are.

Bidding Good Riddance To The Unkempt Teacher

"If you are going to go, Then you need to be gone.

Don't worry 'bout ME, I'll get alone. If you are going to go,

This time stay gone. Don't sing to ME, Another Tired and Broken song.

If you are going to go, Go like the blown away wind,

Dusty footprints in the sands for the same old, new beginning.

Just storm, right, out of MY back door, No left handed wave,

Don't want to see You again, No more. Arms are broken from begging,

Done this before. If you are going to go, Go and keep going.

Peaceful nights are coming, Love's rainy Life will forever be snoring.

www.ingramcontent.com/pod-product-compliance
Lightning Source LLC
LaVergne TN
LVHW040200080526
838202LV00042B/3247